W9-BTZ-862

NO. **001** FROM: _____
DATE: _____

☐ *to share*
☐ *to keep*

THIS BOOK BELONGS TO:

PLEASE RETURN TO OWNER IF BORROWED OR FOUND

WE ARE THE
GARDENERS

JOANNA GAINES
AND KIDS

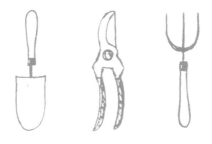

illustrated by
JULIANNA SWANEY

Tommy
NELSON

An Imprint of Thomas Nelson

We Are the Gardeners

© 2019 by Joanna Gaines

Published in Nashville, Tennessee, by Tommy Nelson. Tommy Nelson is an imprint of Thomas Nelson. Thomas Nelson is a registered trademark of HarperCollins Christian Publishing, Inc.

Illustrations by Julianna Swaney

Tommy Nelson titles may be purchased in bulk for educational, business, fund-raising, or sales promotional use. For information, please email SpecialMarkets@ThomasNelson.com.

ISBN-13: 978-1-4003-1422-5

Library of Congress Cataloging-in-Publication Data is on file.

Printed in the United States of America

19 20 21 22 23 WPW 6 5 4 3 2 1
Mfr: WPW / Stevens Point, WI / March 2019 / 9529493

TO OUR DAD:

You have taught us that we can do hard things

and to never give up, even when we fail.

WE ARE THE GARDENERS.

That's a pretty official title, but we didn't start out this way.

Just like our garden, we started small and grew from there. Some

say that a garden just grows from seeds, but we think it grows from

trying and failing and trying again. A garden is hard work,

but so is most of the good, important stuff in life.

Our family's garden story began with one small
potted fern. Dad stumbled upon it at the hardware
store when he ran in for some supplies. He said it
was just too cute to leave behind, and he thought
it would make Mom smile. And it did!

We chose a sunny windowsill for that pretty little fern.
It seemed like a good, safe spot for him to grow. This
was back when we were little kids, but we still remember
visiting the plant each day to give him a drink, and
sometimes we'd even whisper to him a bit.

And then, *PLOT TWIST!* Out of nowhere, our fern died. Death by overhydration. That's just a fancy way of saying we gave him way too much water. Looking back, each one of us must have watered him every day. That's a lot of drinks for a little plant. By mistake, we loved that plant to death. Some people tell themselves they are no good at something after one small failure. But no chance were we going to give up that easily.

So we checked out some books from the library, and we found out that ferns can be tricky and prefer to live in a shady spot. Apparently a plant's leaves can communicate to us what they're needing.

We also learned that most plants have good manners and like to sip, not gulp. Lesson learned!

Dad got us a fresh fern, and with it came FRESH HOPE. This time, we set the pot on our piano, way on the other side of the room, where the sun wouldn't give him so much attention. We made a watering schedule and took turns saying a lot of nice things to our little sprout of a plant. And fern number two lived and thrived and grew, and finally Mom got him a little potted friend.

And then another. And then one or two more. We noticed that talking to our plants actually helped them grow BIGGER and STRONGER, so we added some songs and jokes into the mix. Unlike when we overwatered, zero plants died from us talking too much. Pretty soon, plants were taking over the house, and Dad said it was time to graduate to outdoor gardening.

Mom was as excited about the new outdoor
garden as we were, and she started talking
about it with a DREAMY look in her eyes.
That's when Dad called a family meeting
so we could come up with a real plan.

We all gathered around the kitchen table and got to work dreaming, planning, and drawing things out.

We knew we needed a sunny spot—a place where the plants
could sunbathe for at least six hours a day. We'd be red
as radishes if we did that, but plants just love it.
And more than that, they need it.
In the garden, there is no
life without light.

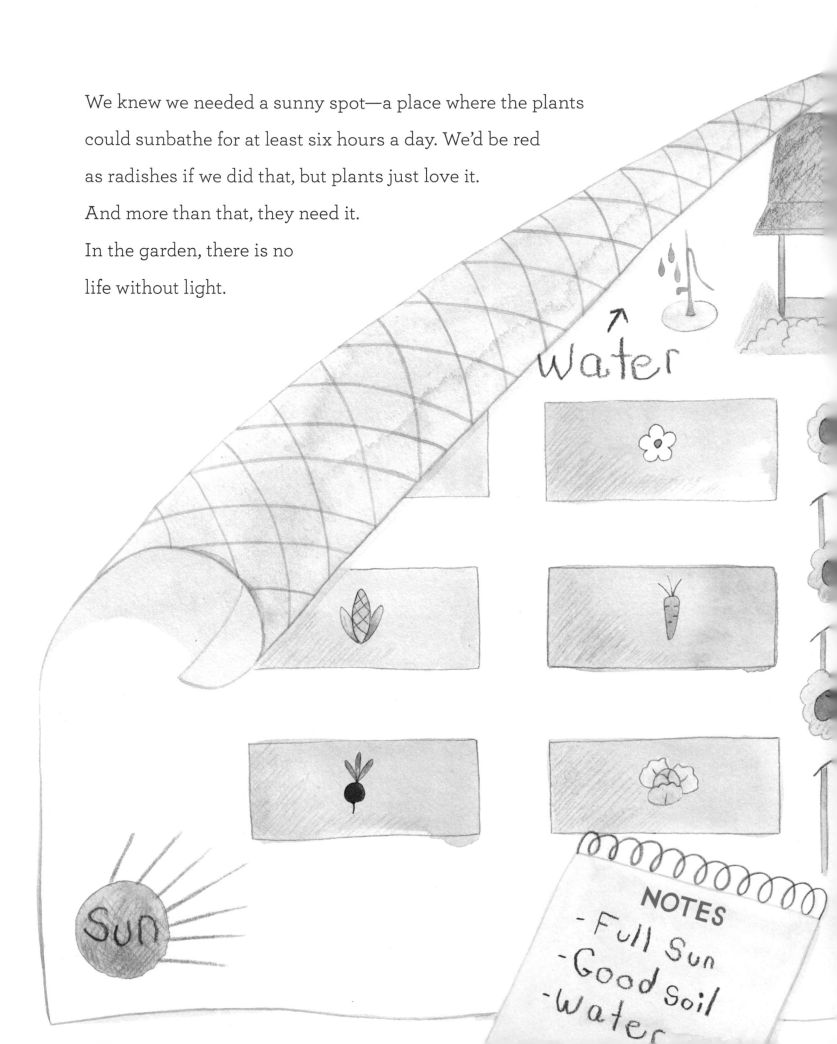

Shed

Chickens

SNAP PEAS

Dad always says that the foundation is the most important thing when it comes to building a house. A house can't be strong if it's built on something weak, and the same holds true in the garden. So to make the foundation of our garden strong, we filled it with something called soil. Good soil—which includes a bunch of tiny living things called organisms—can grow things in it.

That's pretty amazing when you stop and think about it. A whole hidden world of life is happening beneath our feet. Just because you can't see the good things with your eyes doesn't mean they're not there! And another cool thing about soil is that it feeds and strengthens the seeds we sow, and then, *LIKE A MIRACLE,* plants and flowers burst out of the ground!

We also knew we needed our garden to get plenty of water. Rain is the very best thing for plants to drink, but it's hard to know when and if rain is coming. So a couple other options to keep plants hydrated are to collect rainwater or use a sprinkler or garden hose to get the job done.

Once we had a location with plenty of sun, good soil, and a watering plan, we got right to work. First things first: SEEDS! The most fun part of planning out our garden was deciding what to plant. We started with the foods we like to eat, like strawberries and tomatoes, and then we chose some pretty flowers to keep them company. The thing about seeds is that they're EVERYDAY MIRACLES. Everything a plant will grow up to be is already hidden inside the seed.

We chose flowers like zinnias, sunflowers, and cosmos so that pollinators would visit our garden. Butterflies, hummingbirds, and bees spread pollen around from flower to flower, encouraging even more things to bloom. We like knowing that little helpers are out there in nature working with us to help this garden grow.

The bees must have put the word out that we had a pretty good thing going because, sure enough, all sorts of other critters started to arrive. We quickly found out that there were three types of bugs in our backyard:

THE GOOD, THE BAD, AND THE UGLY.

Let's start with the worst part. It was a pretty sad day when the aphids (pronounced ay-fids) arrived. They are some of the more well-known villains in the gardening world—they suck the life right out of plants. But then the ladybugs showed up to eat those pesky aphids for lunch. Ladybugs are for sure part of the hero camp, bravely protecting our plant friends from harm.

And we've gotta tell you about earthworms.

They're like the SECRET AGENTS of the garden. Earthworms eat all of the

dead things, like old roots and leaves, and turn them into life for the soil. Every

time we found one, we would all high-five and celebrate. They aren't pretty,

but who cares? They're awesome, and we love seeing them hard at work.

We realized pretty quickly that we needed to keep
the weeds out. They are the true bullies of the garden.
Weeds try to steal water, sunlight, and nutrients from
our fruits and veggies, and it's our job to make sure
those little rascals don't take over.

If we ignore the garden for too long, the weeds run wild and hurt our beloved plants. It's so much easier to do just a little bit every day.

We were OFFICIALLY gardeners and had a real-life garden to prove it!
That garden became our pride and joy. Day in and day out, we tended
to our plants, making sure they got plenty of sun and water.

Every time a new plant sprouted up from the ground,

our excitement grew right along with it.

As time passed, our garden grew bigger,

AND SO DID OUR FAMILY!

When our garden was finally in full bloom
and growing tall, we'd run through the aisles
and watch the butterflies flutter around us.

But one day, as we were mid-skip, we noticed some trespassers helping themselves to lunch—and by lunch, we mean half of the garden. Animals may look cute and innocent, but some have a sneaky side. They can wipe out a garden in no time flat.

The chickens ate the vegetables. The goats ate Mom's roses. And the bunnies weren't picky at all—they ate anything in sight! Saying good-bye to that many happy plants was even harder than throwing away our very first dead fern. We debated if we should just give up. Was it really worth it to start all over again? Then we remembered one very important detail:

WE ARE THE GARDENERS.

It was our responsibility not only to grow this garden but also to protect it. So we put up a little fence to keep the animals out and got to work rebuilding our garden!

It didn't take long to get our plants and flowers growing tall again. To this day, our very favorite days are when we get to gather the FRUITS OF OUR LABOR. Mom loves to set the table with pretty flowers in every color you can imagine. We help her dream up recipes for the food we've grown.

Sometimes when we see all of that beauty laid out, we can't believe our hands helped bring it to life, and it makes all the hard work worth it. It's what keeps us coming back, day after day, season after season.

We still keep a little fern on the piano to remind us of our small beginnings. Every time we water it, we're reminded not to give up when things don't work out the first time. Because the thing is, whether one potted fern dies or half of the garden is wiped out by little critters, every failure or setback teaches us something. Dad says that every hard thing we choose to do MAKES US BRAVER for the next time.

There are so many lessons waiting
to be learned and a whole world of
gardening ready to bloom . . .

WE ARE THE GARDENERS,

and you can be too!